DATE DUE		
		AUG 3 0 2006	MAY 3 1 2007	
		NOV 3 0 2006		
		NOV 2 6 2010		
		DISCARDED BY THE		
		URBANA FREE LIBRARY		

Put Beginning Readers on the Right Track with
ALL ABOARD READING™

The All Aboard Reading series is especially for beginning readers. Written by noted authors and illustrated in full color, these are books that children really and truly *want* to read—books to excite their imagination, tickle their funny bone, expand their interests, and support their feelings. With four different reading levels, All Aboard Reading lets you choose which books are most appropriate for your children and their growing abilities.

Picture Readers—for Ages 3 to 6
Picture Readers have super-simple texts, with many nouns appearing as rebus pictures. At the end of each book are 24 flash cards—on one side is the rebus picture; on the other side is the written-out word.

Level 1—for Preschool through First-Grade Children
Level 1 books have very few lines per page, very large type, easy words, lots of repetition, and pictures with visual "cues" to help children figure out the words on the page.

Level 2—for First-Grade to Third-Grade Children
Level 2 books are printed in slightly smaller type than Level 1 books. The stories are more complex, but there is still lots of repetition in the text, and many pictures. The sentences are quite simple and are broken up into short lines to make reading easier.

Level 3—for Second-Grade through Third-Grade Children
Level 3 books have considerably longer texts, harder words, and more complicated sentences.

All Aboard for happy reading!

For Mom and Dad—J.F.

To Eli—A.E.

Text copyright © 2001 by Jennifer Frantz. Illustrations copyright © 2001 by Allan Eitzen. All rights reserved. Published by Grosset & Dunlap, a division of Penguin Putnam Books for Young Readers, New York. GROSSET & DUNLAP and ALL ABOARD READING are trademarks of Penguin Putnam Inc. Published simultaneously in Canada. Printed in the U.S.A.

Library of Congress Cataloging-in-Publication Data is available.

ISBN 0-448-42476-2 (GB)   A B C D E F G H I J

ISBN 0-448-42423-1 (pbk.)   A B C D E F G H I

ALL
ABOARD
READING™
Level 2
Grades 1-3

Totem Poles

By Jennifer Frantz
Illustrated by Allan Eitzen

Grosset & Dunlap • New York

The Pacific Northwest, 1750

It is a big day

for the Haida tribe.

Drums beat and voices chant.

People in costumes are dancing.

6

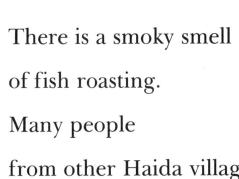

There is a smoky smell
of fish roasting.
Many people
from other Haida villages
are here.
They have come
to help put up a totem pole.

A large hole has been dug

in the ground.

Fifty strong men have been chosen.

They will lift the pole.

Slowly, slowly,

the men raise the pole.

The men take many breaks.

The totem pole is very heavy.

It is hard work.

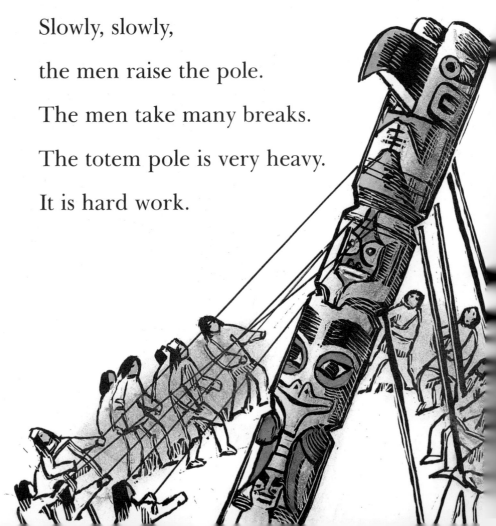

The men must not drop it.

That would be bad luck.

Voices chant louder
and louder.
Then everyone cheers!
The totem pole is
in place.
The totem pole is
sixty feet high.
That's as tall as ten men.

This man made the pole.

His tools hang around his neck.

It took him a year

to make the carvings.

He is proud of his work.

He gets to do a special dance.

Then comes a feast—

a feast called a potlatch.

(You say it like this: POT-lach)

A potlatch may last for many days.

It is held for big events in a tribe—

like weddings or births.

The potlatch shows people

from other Haida clans

that this family is rich and powerful.

The host family has made
fancy plates, bowls, and trays
just for the feast.

There are gifts for all the guests.

The gifts must be very special.

They also show that the family

is rich and powerful.

So does the totem pole.

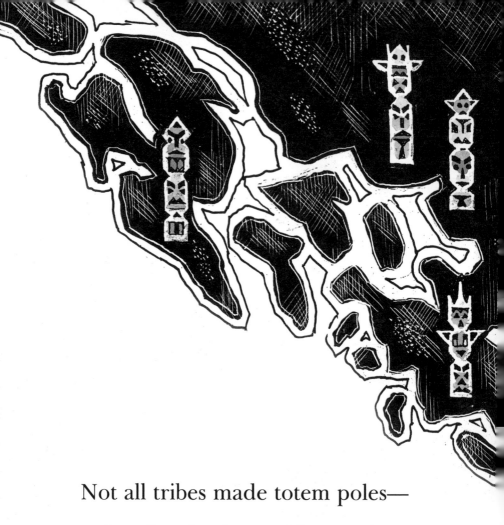

Not all tribes made totem poles—

only tribes in the Pacific Northwest.

You can see this area on the map.

Many tribes settled here.

The land was rich

with plants and animals.

So were the rivers and the sea.

People fished for salmon
and they hunted sea lions.

They also hunted deer and bear.

They used animal skins

to make clothes.

They used trees
to build houses and fires.

They also used trees
to make totem poles.
They were carved
from red cedar trees.

An old legend says that the first
totem pole came from the sea.
Have you ever seen driftwood?
The knots and twists can
look like faces or animals.
Sometimes driftwood looks like
it has been carved by a person.
Driftwood may have given people
the idea to make totem poles.

Carvers used simple tools
like axes and chisels.
They were made of shells, stone,
wood, and animal bones and teeth.

Many totem poles were painted.

The paints were made

from crushed rocks and plants.

It could take a whole year

to make one pole.

Each totem pole told a story.

The animals on the pole

were part of the story.

One Haida legend was about

a young man and a killer whale.

The man's name was Nanasimget.

(You say it like this: nan-AH-sim-jit.)

One day,

his wife was by the water.

All at once,

a killer whale rose up.

It grabbed her and took her far below.

The whale wanted to make her his bride.

Nanasimget dove in
after her.
He found where
the whale lived.
He spilled
a pot of water
onto the fire.
Steam filled the room.
Nanasimget found
his wife and they fled.
She was saved.

This pole retells
the legend
of Nanasimget
in pictures.
Do you see
the whale?
What else
do you see?

The Haida did not have books.

Totem poles were a way

that stories could be passed on.

Totem poles also kept track

of a family's history.

The Haida people had two main groups—
the Eagles and the Ravens.

Look at this totem pole.

It belongs to the Eagle group.

Do you see the eagle

on top of the pole?

In each main group,

there were smaller groups—

or families.

Each family had its own animal.

One family might pick

the beaver.

The beaver would appear

on all of their totem poles.

Do you see the beaver?

Sometimes families had

more than one animal.

If they beat an enemy

they took on that animal, too.

If a man from a beaver family

married a woman from a frog family,

then their pole could have a beaver

and a frog on it.

The animals were passed down

in the family.

The totem poles were

like a coat of arms.

They told who the family was.

Totem poles were also used

to mark off land—

kind of like flags.

Totem poles always faced

the shoreline.

This is because people

traveled by canoe.

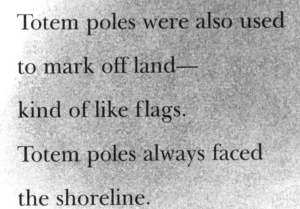

When visitors got to the shore,

they saw a totem pole.

They knew that people lived there.

Some poles had watchmen
on the very top.
These poles were on the front
of Haida houses.
The watchmen
were to keep the house safe.

Sometimes totem poles were put up

in honor of dead chiefs.

Some even held the ashes

of the dead person.

There were also "shame poles."
They were to embarrass
people in the tribe—
people who did not pay debts.

Many of the old totem poles have
worn away over time.

Today, there are new totem pole carvers.

They try to keep the old way alive.

They pass down the art
and stories of totem poles,
just as others did long ago.